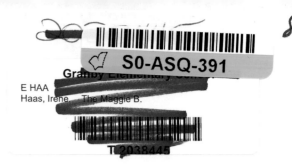

THE MAGGIE B.

THE MAGGIE B.

BY IRENE HAAS

Aladdin Books
Macmillan Publishing Company
New York

For Jo and for Jim
who helped make this book.

Aladdin Books
Macmillan Publishing Company
866 Third Avenue, New York, NY 10022
Collier Macmillan Canada, Inc.

First Aladdin edition

Printed in the United States of America

A hardcover edition of *The Maggie B.* is available from Atheneum.

5   4   3   2

Library of Congress Cataloging-in-Publication Data

Haas, Irene.
  The Maggie B.
  (Aladdin books)

  Summary: A little girl's wish to sail for a day on a
boat named for her "with someone nice for company"
comes true.
  [1. Boats and boating—Fiction.   2. Wishes—Fiction]
I. Title.
PZ7.H1128mag   1987   [E]   86-31176
ISBN 0-689-70764-9 (pbk.)

THE MAGGIE B.

This is a story
of a wish come true.
Margaret Barnstable
wished on a star one night—

North Star, star of the sea,
I wish for a ship
Named after me,
To sail for a day
Alone and free,
With someone nice
For company.

And then she went
off to bed.

When she woke up, she was in the cabin of her own ship.
It was named *The Maggie B.* after her, and the nice company
was her brother, James, who was a dear baby.

A rooster crowed on deck, so Margaret knew the day was
about to begin. She took James out to welcome the sun. It
warmed them up and brightened the sky.

On the poop deck was a tiny farm.

There were a goat and some chickens, an apple tree
and a peach tree and an orange tree with a toucan
perched on a branch. They picked an orange for breakfast.

Since it was her own little cabin, in her own little ship, Margaret worked hard and tidied it up with a joyful hustle-bustle.

All the sparkling morning, while she scrubbed the deck
and made the ship ready to sail, she sang an old sea chantey.

Oh the sailor's life is bold and free,
His home is on the rolling sea.
Y'heave ho, my lads, come sail with me.

The Maggie B. was soon riding the tops of the waves like a bird.

In the early afternoon, Margaret and James had
a picnic lunch under the apple tree.
"What shall we have for supper tonight?" Margaret
wondered, as soon as lunch was over.
With a lovely idea in her mind, she gathered a basketful
of delicious things from the farm.
And out of the sea she netted a blue-green lobster and a
silvery sea bass.

On her little stove, Margaret set a big pot of broth to bubble and boil. She chop-chop-chopped the vegetables and put them into the pot, and then in went the sweet-smelling herbs, the gleaming, glistening fish and the knobby, hard-shelled lobster.

As she whipped off her apron, she closed her eyes and breathed in the smell of the good sea stew. All afternoon it would simmer and fill the air with its fragrance.

The Maggie B. sailed steadily on.
The breeze was gentle, warm and soft.
James had his nap on a velvet pillow,
and Margaret painted a handsome
portrait of him.

After juice-and-cookie time, she gave James his counting
lesson, and this is how she did it.

One, two, three, four, five,
Once I caught a fish alive.
Six, seven, eight, nine, ten,
But I let him go again.
Why did you let him go?
Because he bit my finger so.
Which finger did he bite?
The little one upon the right.

And she gave James' little finger a nibble, which
made him laugh and laugh—until suddenly he stopped.

The sun had disappeared!

Margaret and James were cold.
The sky grew darker.
The goat and chickens fled
into their little shelter,
the toucan flew screeching
into the cabin.
James started to cry.
A storm was coming!
Margaret must make
the boat ready at once.

She took in the sail and tied it tight. She dropped
the anchor and stowed all the gear, while rain drummed
on the deck and thunder rumbled above her.

Lightning split the sky as she ran into the cabin and
slammed the door against the wet wind.
Now everything was safe and secure.

When she lit the lamps, the cabin was bright and warm.
It was nearly suppertime so Margaret mixed up a batch
of muffins and slid them into the oven. She sliced some
peaches and put cinnamon and honey on top, and they
went into the oven, too.

James was given a splashy bath in the sink. Margaret
dried him in a big, warm towel, and then supper was ready.

Outside, the wind howled like a pack of hungry wolves. Rain lashed the windowpanes. But the sturdy little *Maggie B.* kept her balance and only rocked the nicest little bit.

Margaret and James ate the beautiful sea stew and dunked their muffins in the broth, which tasted of all the good things that had cooked in it. For dessert they had the peaches with cinnamon and honey, and glasses of warm goat's milk.

When supper was over,
Margaret played old tunes
on her fiddle. Then she rocked
James in his cradle and sang
him her favorite song.

Sweet and low, sweet and low,
Wind of the western sea.
Low, low breathe and blow,
Wind of the western sea!
Over the rolling waters go,
Come from the dying moon
And blow.
Blow him again to me,
While my little one,
While my pretty one
Sleeps.

Margaret tucked in the baby's covers and took a last
look out at the night.

The storm was not an angry one anymore. Nice steady
rain made a lullaby sound on the roof of the cabin.

So Margaret got into her bunk. She blew out her lamp,
curled up inside her nest of blankets and fell asleep.

The day on *The Maggie B.* was over.